Happy reading!

Jamie Rutherford
2024

Miles and the Wren House Toad

Written and illustrated by
Jamie Ruthenberg

ISBN-13: 978-0692704509

ISBN-10: 0692704507

For Gracie

It was an early spring morning
when Miles sniffed the cool breeze
that swept across his mother's
lettuce patch.

He felt cheerful this morning for it was finally spring and he was picking baby lettuce to make a bouquet for his mother.

This was Miles' favorite time of year, when the garden came to life again. A fresh green blanket covered the yard as plants peeked from the ground.

The birds started to tweet and chirp as they built their nests, and the maples and oaks were sprinkled with new baby leaves.

As Miles walked back to the house, he could see the birdhouse in the distance. Mama called it the wren house, because it was a little house made for a tiny songbird called a wren.

As Miles got closer, he saw
something in the wren house,
and it wasn't a wren.

It wasn't even a bird!

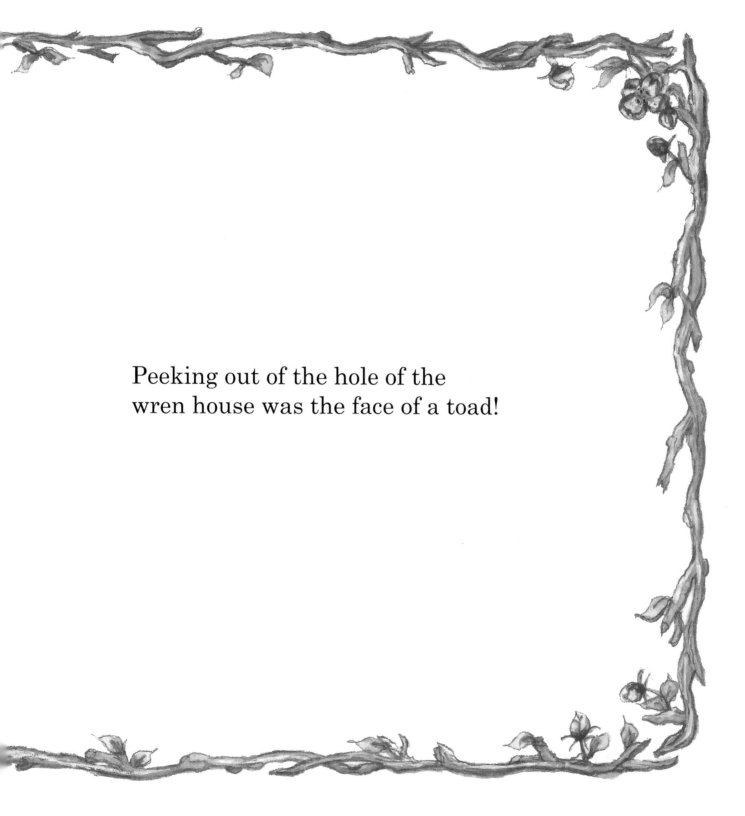

Peeking out of the hole of the
wren house was the face of a toad!

Miles walked to the base of the
wren house and looked straight
up.

The toad carefully climbed out of the
hole and peeked over
the birdhouse deck
and down at Miles.

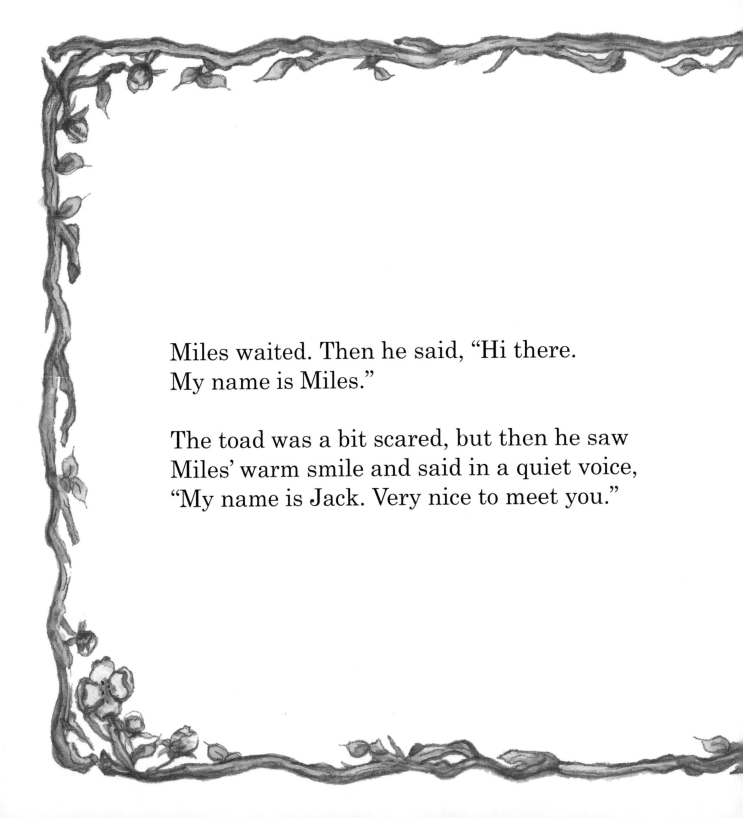

Miles waited. Then he said, "Hi there.
My name is Miles."

The toad was a bit scared, but then he saw
Miles' warm smile and said in a quiet voice,
"My name is Jack. Very nice to meet you."

"It is very nice to meet you, too," Miles said.
"I haven't seen anyone in this birdhouse
since last summer. She was a wren with
three little babies. Once the babies left the
nest, she moved and never came back."

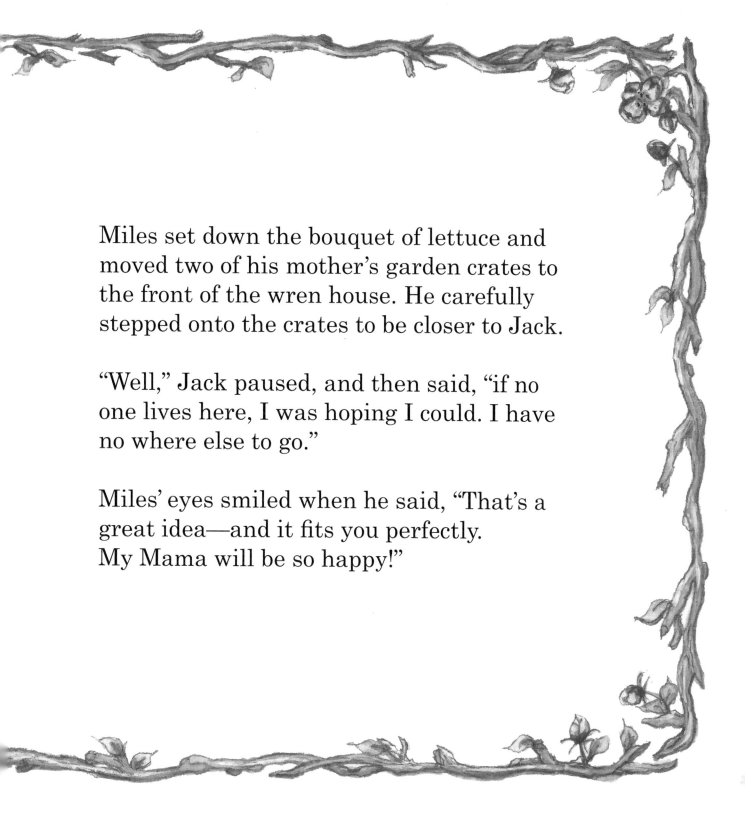

Miles set down the bouquet of lettuce and moved two of his mother's garden crates to the front of the wren house. He carefully stepped onto the crates to be closer to Jack.

"Well," Jack paused, and then said, "if no one lives here, I was hoping I could. I have no where else to go."

Miles' eyes smiled when he said, "That's a great idea—and it fits you perfectly. My Mama will be so happy!"

Just then, Chip and Charlotte came racing from the back of the yard. Charlotte was chasing Chip in a game of tag. Suddenly, Chip stopped next to Miles. "What are you up to, Pal?" asked Chip.

He quickly looked up at Jack, and
before Miles could answer, Chip
started laughing. "A toad in a
birdhouse? That's funny!"

"You're it!" yelled Charlotte as she
tagged Chip's arm.

"No way!" said Chip, and they
both darted around and around
in circles and then to the back
of the yard once again.

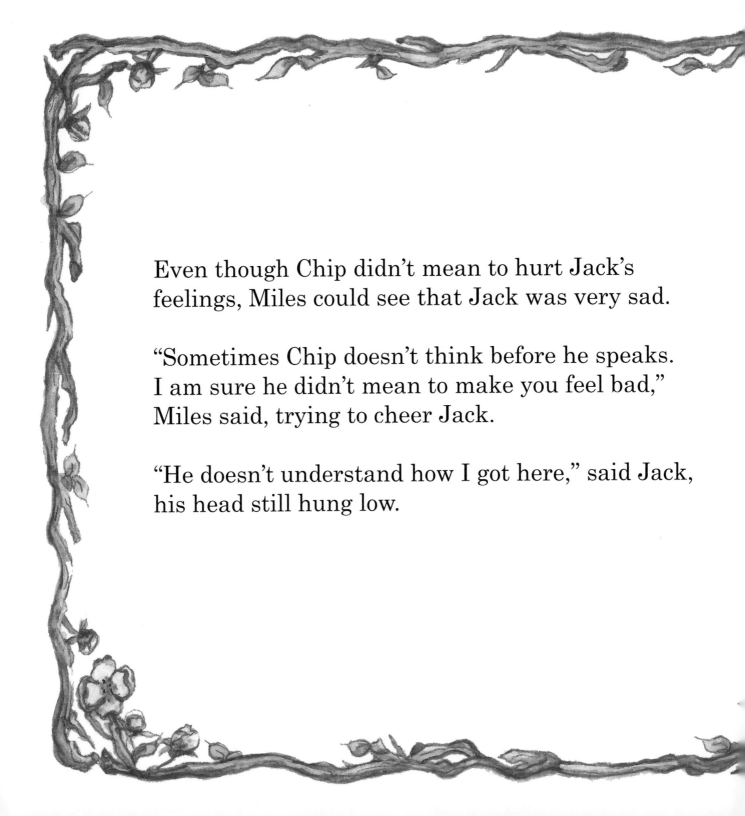

Even though Chip didn't mean to hurt Jack's feelings, Miles could see that Jack was very sad.

"Sometimes Chip doesn't think before he speaks. I am sure he didn't mean to make you feel bad," Miles said, trying to cheer Jack.

"He doesn't understand how I got here," said Jack, his head still hung low.

"Hmmmm, how can I help Chip understand that he hurt Jack's feelings?" thought Miles.

Miles had an idea.

Miles found his favorite pencil and a piece of paper from his special notebook, and he wrote as Jack told his story. Not long before, Jack was just a tadpole and he had yet to learn how to write his ABC's, so Miles offered to write the words for him.

A Toad's Journey by Jack

There once was a tadpole that lived in a pond. He loved living with his family in the cool water.

One day, the tadpole woke up to find that everyone was gone! He looked and saw his friends crawling out of the pond. Then he saw they were not tadpoles anymore. They looked like little toads!

He swam up and took his first steps out of the water. The breeze blew against his skin and the grass felt cold and stiff. He knew to be careful of the snakes in the grass and the owls above for they were dangerous. The worried toad started looking for a safe place to go.

He searched and searched. Then he spotted something wooden up on a tall post, and it had a small hole into which he could crawl. The little toad climbed up and in. Although he felt lonely, he was glad to finally find a place where he could rest and feel safe.

The End

(The toad in this story is me, Jack. This is my real-life story.)

Miles walked to the old oak where
Chip lived, and asked him to read
Jack's story. Chip read the story carefully.

Being a kind squirrel at heart, Chip now
understood why Jack was in the wren house.
He realized that he wasn't thinking of
Jack's feelings when he first saw him.

That morning, Chip walked over to
the wren house and apologized to Jack.

When he said, "I am sorry,
Jack," he really meant it.

It was soon afternoon, and Mama was making her carrot cake. She always had extra cream cheese frosting in a little bowl just for Miles.

Mama's big bouquet of lettuce stood tall on the kitchen table. Miles nibbled from it as he, Chip, and Jack helped Mama measure spices and stir batter.

Even though there wasn't much for a toad to eat in Mama's kitchen, Jack had a nibble of lettuce and was surprised at how much he liked it. Then, he licked a big spoon of white, fluffy frosting. "This is the best thing I ever tasted!"

"I didn't know toads ate frosting," said Chip with a silly giggle.

"I didn't either!" said Jack, and they both held their bellies as they laughed.

The End

Hi again!

I am writing you a letter (I love writing letters) because I really want to hear what you think!
- Did something like this ever happen to you? What happened?
- My friends and I had many feelings throughout this story. What were some of those feelings? Did you ever feel that way, too?

Sometimes stories are like other stories.
- Did you ever read a story like this one?
- What was the story? How are they alike?

I can't wait to write you again soon!
Your friend,
Miles

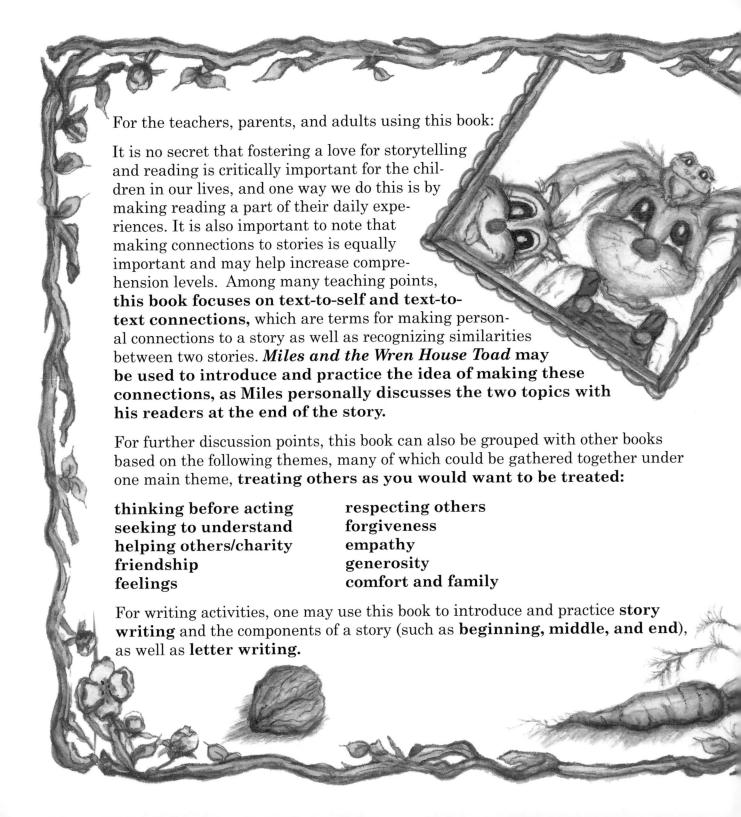

For the teachers, parents, and adults using this book:

It is no secret that fostering a love for storytelling and reading is critically important for the children in our lives, and one way we do this is by making reading a part of their daily experiences. It is also important to note that making connections to stories is equally important and may help increase comprehension levels. Among many teaching points, **this book focuses on text-to-self and text-to-text connections,** which are terms for making personal connections to a story as well as recognizing similarities between two stories. *Miles and the Wren House Toad* **may be used to introduce and practice the idea of making these connections, as Miles personally discusses the two topics with his readers at the end of the story.**

For further discussion points, this book can also be grouped with other books based on the following themes, many of which could be gathered together under one main theme, **treating others as you would want to be treated:**

thinking before acting   **respecting others**
seeking to understand   **forgiveness**
helping others/charity   **empathy**
friendship   **generosity**
feelings   **comfort and family**

For writing activities, one may use this book to introduce and practice **story writing** and the components of a story (such as **beginning, middle, and end**), as well as **letter writing.**

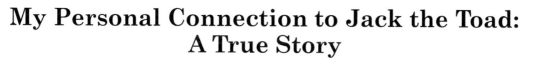

My Personal Connection to Jack the Toad: A True Story

Years ago, I was working in my rose garden during a sunny summer afternoon. Near my garden was an old birdhouse made especially for a wren (a little songbird). That afternoon, I was walking past the wren house when I suddenly saw a little face peak out of it—and it wasn't a wren. It wasn't even a bird!

It was a toad!

A small, grey American toad was living in my wren house. I laughed to myself and called for my daughter to come and look at our new neighbor. She ran up, looked at him closely with a big smile as he stared back at her, and declared, "His name is Jack!" From that point on, he was Jack the Toad.

Jack lived in the house for three years, and, in fact, one summer, he even had a friend live with him in that little birdhouse.

I am not sure where he went after those three summers—maybe to a more spacious birdhouse with more amenities. Nonetheless, I miss him greatly…

Truly, this real-life connection of mine is an example of how life can sometimes be more interesting than fiction. Don't you think?

—Jamie Ruthenberg

Jack and his friend sunbathing on the front porch of the wren house—I had to take a picture. They slept in the sun for two hours that lazy, summer afternoon, and then woke to watch me work in the rose garden.

About the Author

Jamie Ruthenberg is a Detroit-born author and illustrator. As a certified teacher in elementary education and a long-time professional writer, today she lives in Clarkston, Michigan with her daughter.

Jamie has been sketching the character of Miles since she was a small child. Many years later, with watercolor and pencil, she has developed him into a kindhearted and thoughtful soul that treats other with love and respect, even during challenging circumstances. He is truly a character with integrity that treats others as he would want to be treated.

by Jamie
Ruthenberg
AUTHOR / ILLUSTRATOR

Artist's note:

The paintings for this book were created with pencil and watercolor.
The text was set in Century Schoolbook.

If you enjoyed this book by Jamie Ruthenberg, you and your family may also enjoy another one of her delightful stories!

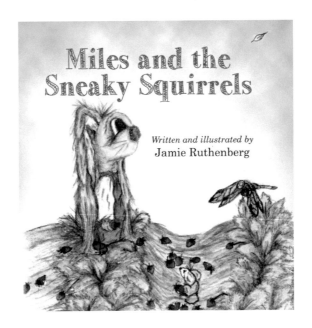

Paperback ISBN: 978-0692486054
Available for purchase at:
JamieRuthenberg.com

Made in the USA
Columbia, SC
12 June 2024

36829880R00027